Kitten Kitty
Reads a Book

Story by Gene G. Bradbury

Illustrated by Jean Wyatt

BookWilde Children's Books

Kitten Kitty Reads a Book

ISBN: 978-0-9971764-5-2

Illustrations by Jean Wyatt

Book prepress: Kate Weisel, weiselcreative.com

All inquiries should be addressed to

BookWilde Children's Books

422 Williamson Rd.

Sequim, WA 98382

www.genegbradbury.com

Printed in the United States

BookWilde Children's Books

Author's Dedication

Dedicated to our dog, Little Ann, who loved to chase cats.

~ Gene G. Bradbury

Illustrator's Dedication

Dedicated to Foxy and Lionel, two very lovable and inspiring cats.

~ Jean Wyatt

Come Kitten Kitty
in warm pajamas,
socks on paws,
don't forget . . .
your storybook.

Kitten Kitty
on Mama's lap.

"We'll read a story
before your nap."

See elephants bathing,

monkeys on a swing.
Did I hear the doorbell ring?

A friend is at the door
in warm pajamas, socks on paws,

make room for . . .
one kitten more.

Oh, my kittens,
see lions sunning,

birds that sing.
Did I hear the doorbell ring?

Another friend is at the door
in warm pajamas, socks on paws,

make room for . . .
one kitten more.

Look, my kittens,
see flamingoes dancing

before their king.
Did I hear the doorbell ring?

How many kittens
can one lap hold?
One, two, three, maybe four.

At the window Mama sees
more kittens with storybooks
at the door.

Can one lap hold more than four?

Mama finishes the storybook.
She hears the sound of many feet.

Where have all the kittens

gone?

One kitten is left
in warm pajamas,
socks on paws.
Who is the kitten?

Mama knows. . .

Kitten Kitty is fast asleep.

ALL ABOUT CATS and KITTENS

1.   Cats are very ancient animals and go back millions of years.

2.   Cats are very popular because they are both independent and affectionate.

3.   Playing with kittens keeps them healthy and alert, and teaches them skills as well.

4.   Kittens love to climb and hide. Make your own cat center using cardboard boxes.

5.   There are hundreds of kinds of kittens. You may know a Siamese, Persian, or Bengal.

6.   Kittens talk to us not only by meowing, but by their body language.

7.   If your kitten's tail is up and she is walking toward you, she may be saying, "Hello."

8.   A kitten may rub against your legs to say, "Pay attention to me."

9.   When a kitten says "Hello," it is best to tickle the kitten's head.

10.   A kitten stretched out on its side is relaxed.

11.   A kitten crouched with her tail beneath her and her eyes wide is saying, "I'm scared."

12.   A kitten arching his back with his fur standing on end is fearful.

13.   A kitten depends upon his humans for regular checkups, vaccinations, and feeding.

14.   All kittens require water and a good diet of cat food.

15.   Ask your parents about having your cat "neutered." This procedure, done by a veterinarian, can make your cat healthier and happier.

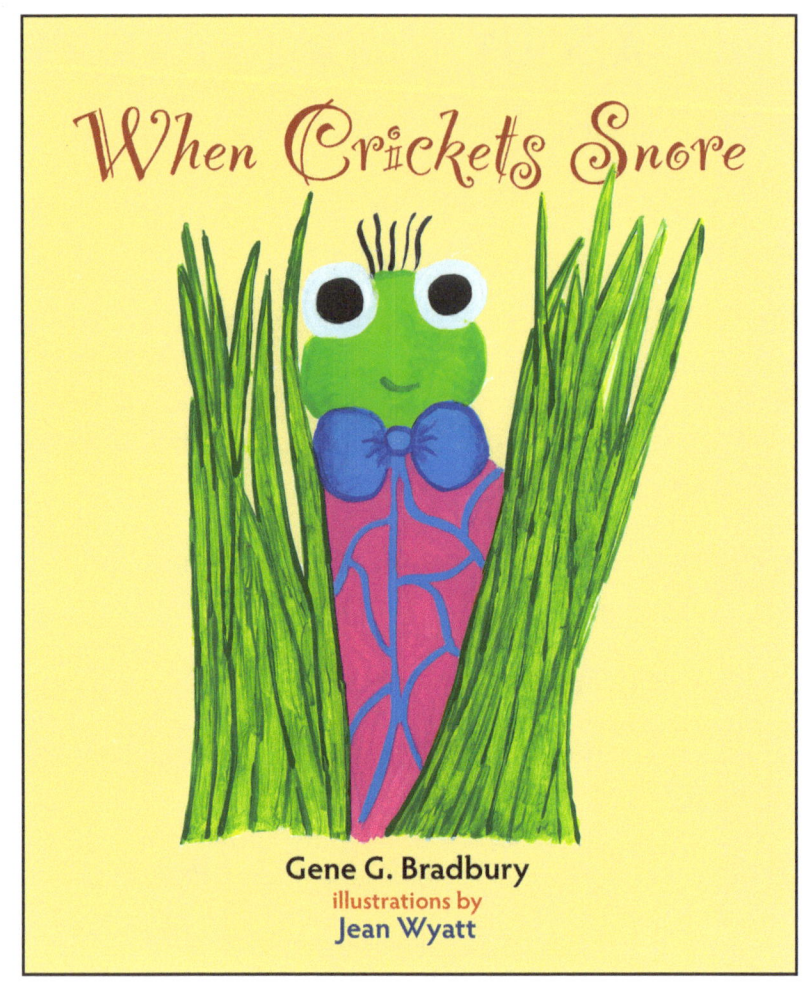

When Crickets Snore

Gene G. Bradbury
illustrations by
Jean Wyatt

Have you read
"When Crickets Snore"?

by Gene G. Bradbury
and
illustrated by Jean Wyatt

BookWilde Children's Books

Children's Books by the Author

These books are illustrated by watercolorist Victoria Wickell-Stewart.

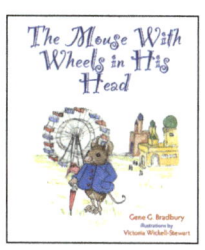

THE MOUSE WITH WHEELS IN HIS HEAD: Meet Fergus who wants to be the first mouse to ride the new Ferris Wheel at the World's Fair. Can a tiny mouse find a way to hitch a ride without being discovered? Follow Fergus's adventure at the 1893 Chicago Exhibition.

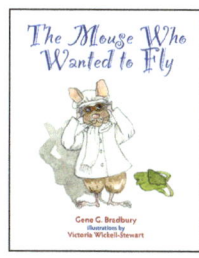

THE MOUSE WHO WANTED TO FLY: Adventure is in Fergus's blood. His success in riding the Ferris Wheel is in the past. When Fergus learns that two brothers, Orville and Wilbur, are going to fly the first powered airplane, Fergus is eager for a new adventure. Is it possible that a mouse can be on the first flight at Kitty Hawk?

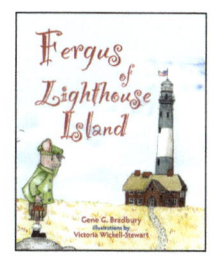

FERGUS OF LIGHTHOUSE ISLAND: Fergus, unlike his great uncle, isn't brave at all. He isn't looking for adventure. But when a hurricane threatens Lighthouse Island, adventure finds him. What will Fergus decide when the hurricane threatens the residents of Mouse Village? It's no place for a mouse who is afraid.

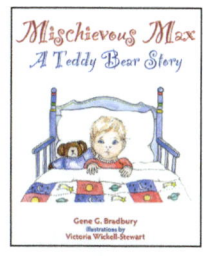

MISCHIEVOUS MAX, A TEDDY BEAR STORY: In Leon's room you will find many teddy bears. Most of them are soft and wonderful to take to bed. But there is one bear who Leon never takes to bed. His name is Max Bear and his fur tickles and his eyes are beastly. Leon knows something else about Max Bear. What if Leon tries sleeping with Max Bear for just one night? Would that be so bad? Leon is about to find out.

THE STAR TREE: "Do the forest animals know about Christmas?" asks Jody. With her grandfather, Jody goes into the forest to the place where the animals gather on Christmas Eve. Jody discovers that the world is a beautiful place to live. The Star Tree invites children to look for Christmas in the natural world.

THE KING'S BUTTERFLY invites children to enjoy and respect the beautiful Monarch Butterfly. When the King and Queen capture the butterfly to keep it for a royal pet, they soon find out that a butterfly is meant to fly free. Will they set the butterfly free that it might return again the next year? Perhaps Wizdrop the Wizard has the answer.

FERGUS OF 221B BAKER STREET *and The Case of Hickory, Dickory, Dock:* Haven't you always wanted to know why the mouse ran up the clock? Of course, it's a mystery. When Fergus, the adventuresome mouse, visits his uncle in England he comes to the right place. Uncle Delbert lives behind the walls of the very house where Sherlock Holmes, the famous detective, lives. With his deerstalker hat and Mr. Homes' magnifying glass, Fergus sets out to solve the mystery. But there is one thing Fergus does not count on.

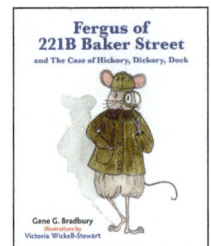

WHEN CRICKETS SNORE is a delightful look at the private life of those singing crickets. It's based on what Henry David Thoreau tells us . . .

In the morning the crickets snore, in the afternoon they chirp, at midnight they dream.

Do they really snore? Page through the lovely illustrations by Jean Wyatt and see for yourself. But read quietly, as the crickets may be in their pajamas.

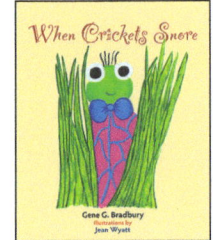

These books are for 7 to 10 year olds.

CLOUD CLIMBER: What were his parents thinking, leaving him for three boring weeks at his grandparent's farm? There would be no internet or cable television and what was worse, only Cousin Emily for company. But on a trip to town with his grandfather, Seth learns of Three Friends Hill and the Banshee's Cave. Are these linked to the discovery of a giant kite Seth and Emily find in the old barn? The three weeks literally fly past and the cousins find that Boring Farm is not so boring after all. Illustrated by Hannah Bradbury.

BEDTIME STORIES TO MAKE YOU SMILE: Bedtime Stories To Make You Smile is the first in a series of bedtime books for young children. In this collection of seven stories the intent is to bring a smile to the reader and send them to sleep with happy dreams. Meet William, a bee who doesn't want to be a bee, and Mr. Mouse who loves to read. You will puzzle over what Leonard has in his box, and delight when you hear of Willie Snooze's special pillows. Aunt Bessie's Elephants may scare you, but just a little. You'll find Boxcar Basset hurtling down the tracks, but not alone. A goldfish tale illustrates that safe driving has benefits for everyone. Illustrated by Hannah Bradbury.

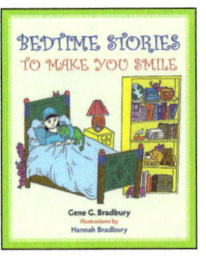

SHORT STORIES UNDER FOUR FEET is a gift before bedtime. All the stories in this selection are short enough to read before going to sleep. None of them are over four pages and can slip easily under a pillow or on a dresser or table. Put on your pajamas and find out how a tree becomes the universe and how a dog, called Lion, brings chaos to the kitchen. Perhaps you would rather read about dancing with Orcas or making pretzels. It's all found between these pages.

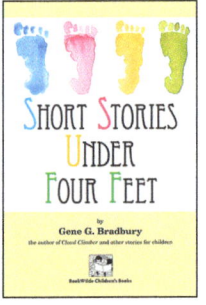

FACES FROM A BROKEN STAR, Short Stories

There was a time when traveling across country one might pull into any small town in America and find a mom and pop cafe. It was a good place to order a fried chicken dinner. Farmers gathered there to compare crop prices and check the weather before working in the field. The local café has disappeared. In these stories you're invited to meet the regulars at the Broken Star Cafe. Some of the characters may sound familiar. Others who will make you laugh and cry.

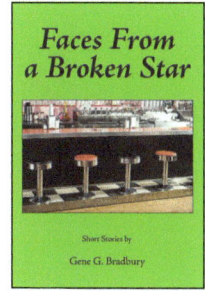

Poetry Books by Gene G. Bradbury

TRAVELING IN COMPANY

We never travel on our journey alone, but are linked by birth to others. They have walked before us and we follow in their footsteps. Those we come to know best on our travels we call family. From them we learn how to live. Others we meet along the way may lead us to quiet paths of reflection and spiritual practice. In this book of poems the author invites us to look at the many ways we are influenced by others as we travel together.

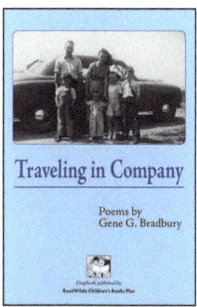

QUIET PLACES, MORNING WALKS:

Notes Between Secular and Sacred

In this book of poetry the author invites the reader to find time each day for quiet and reflection. Each poem is a poetic response to a Psalm verse. The Psalm itself is rewritten in haiku. The book of poetry is prefaced with *morning litanies* to begin the day. The book ends with *evening songs* to end the day. The collection of verse can be used in the morning or evening as a time of quiet and devotion.

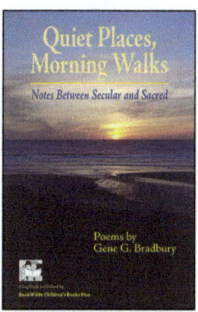

SAUNTERING WITH THOREAU

These poems begin with the author's love of Henry David Thoreau's Journals. Each poem is a reflection on a single quote by Thoreau. The poetry is a brief walk with the nineteenth century naturalist through the woods and along the rivers of Concord. Each poem invites the reader to look intently at the things around them and appreciate the place where they live. In Thoreau's words we are invited to find the kernel of life and not just the husk.

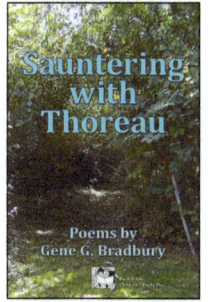

LET ME BE YOUR SERVANT, 100 REFLECTIVE MOMENTS

is both memoir and devotional reading. The book contains 100 short readings from long years of service in parish ministry, hospital chaplaincy, police chaplaincy, prison chaplaincy, and college chaplaincy. Each page reveals the author's choice of reading and thoughts about what it means to live in family and community.

BookWilde Children's Books

All books available at Amazon.com
or barnesandnoble.com

www.ingramcontent.com/pod-product-compliance
Lightning Source LLC
Chambersburg PA
CBHW041003170626
46815CB00002B/143